Leap Year Day

Other Books by Maxine Chernoff

Leap
Year
Day

New and Selected Poems by
Maxine Chernoff

Another Chicago Press

Published by ACP, Box 11223, Chicago, IL 60611

Cover design by Raymond Machura

Cover painting, John la Farge, *Snowy Field, Morning, Roxbury*, 1864, oil on bevelled mahogany panel, 12 x 9⅞ in., gift of Mrs Frank L. Sulzberger in memory of Frank L. Sulzberger, 1981.287...© 1989 The Art Institute of Chicago, All Rights Reserved.

Funded in part with grants from the Illinois Arts Council and the National Endowment for the Arts

Some of these poems first appeared in the following books and chapbooks: *The Last Aurochs* (Now Books, 1976), *A Vegetable Emergency* (Beyond Baroque Foundation, 1977), *Utopia TV Store* (The Yellow Press, 1979), *New Faces of 1952* (Ithaca House, 1985), *Japan* (Avenue B Press, 1987), *Up Late: American Poetry Since 1970* (4 Walls 8 Windows, 1987), and *Cradle and All: Women Writers on Pregnancy and Birth* (Faber & Faber, 1989). And some appeared in the following journals: *The Antioch Review, The Paris Review, Caliban, Sun, Epoch, B-City, Oink!, Broadway 2, Leica Journal, New Langton Catalog, Black Ice, Mirage, Brilliant Corners, Lucky Star, Chicago Poetry Letter News.*

Thanks to my publishers: John Mort; James Krusoe; Richard Friedman, Peter Kostakis, Darlene Pearlstein; John Latta; and Stephen Ratcliffe.

ISBN 0-929968-11-5

Library of Congress Catalog Card Number: 90-80553

Distributed by ILPA, Box 816, Oak Park IL 60303

Contents

New Poems

For Paul

from

A Vegetable Emergency

The Dead Letter Office

Wistfulness covers the windows like drapes. Ten men armed with hankies sort the mail into two categories, letters that make them happy, letters that make them sad. Don't get me wrong. These civil servants, trusted with the awesome duty of burning millions of letters a year, do not open the envelopes like a mortician prying into the life of a client. It is the envelope itself that makes them sad. Childish handwriting scrawled to a deceased aunt makes them weep. A letter from overseas to a wife who has moved, unknown to her husband, creates such tumult that the walls quiver like jelly. Few letters are happy ones, the eviction notice never delivered, the lost bill. But when a happy letter does come into their possession, it's a red letter day. The men cheer wildly, tear up letters, and toss them out of the window, tickertape fashion. And what bliss when something intervenes and a doomed letter, like a terminally ill patient, is saved.

A Sense Of Humor

A lion won't attack if you have a sense of humor. Deadly
canines become child's colored clay, angry claws, so
many handshakes. So you embrace him, careful not to
fall from the celluloid cliff that the two of you call home.
Before he was a pirate who could make you walk a
transparent plank. Now he is your neighbor, attentive to
his topiary garden. Of course this happens in a dream in
which an alligator is dashed against an island like a por-
celain teacup. Of course it is the lion with the *real* sense
of humor. Seeing a woman in a leopard coat, he breaks
from his diamond-studded leash. With his paws upon
her shoulders, he greets her like a favorite aunt or a college roommate, the practical joker. The woman falls to
the ground, her lips a panicky smear. The lion crouches
at the curb, a taxi with a broken meter.

A Birth

"We must seek bodies for our children."
—Osage Indian chant

I can't remember the birth. Cold white rooms, cleanliness the color of nothing. Sometimes a woman dreams that she's given birth to a litter of piglets attached to her breasts like pink balloons. When I look in the crib there is no baby; when I look on the stove there is a pot of soup which was not there before. Sometimes there is a mix-up at the hospital. A patient orders French onion soup and receives cream of shrimp. Sometimes there is a mix-up; a woman receives a child who grows up hating her. One night at a theater a person walks out of the screen and sits down beside her. That is her child, she knows. "The soup is ready," my husband repeats. Silently we sit down side by side. Silently we share one bowl and then another.

The Horizontal Brigade

In the old days the horizontal brigade won every battle.
They had weapons causing death more exotic than
cobra bites, but they never used them. Their music,
played while hiding behind anything horizontal (fallen
oaks, divans, abandoned carriages), was their strength;
charmed horses would offer their glittering manes as
booty when so tantalized. Foxholes were their doll
houses and so they were lovingly guarded. It was only in
emergencies that they called up the reserves, the in-
famous ponies immune to gravity that bombed the club-
foot tanks. Veteran drivers surrendered more out of
novelty than fear. Only once, at the famous Battle of the
Twirling Mists, were they known to use the ultimate
weapons, the costumes that rendered them vertical yet
fierce. Today we are surprised that such men could have
existed. It is like imagining the Age of Reason, when
bearded philosophers drowned in gold bathtubs under
the magnetic gaze of admiring disciples.

On My Birthday

Words line up like racehorses at a starting gate. Nose to nose they edge toward the climactic period. All want to be part of the last line where the reader's gaze will stop, blink, and refocus like a dutiful traffic light. Where do they come from? Like mushrooms they grow in the dark or in clumsy patches, unsightly as warts. Sometimes I try to scare them away; I tell them stories of the pyromaniac, emphasizing the sting of the match. I speak of oblivion as if it were our corner store or the direction the wind will inevitably blow. I tell them they're no better than laundry hanging on the line— that any minute it will rain. Sometimes I threaten to starve them. They're not afraid. They form a column thin as a pencil or the row of numbers a first-grader might add. Today I appeal to their sympathy. "It's my birthday. I want peace." In no time they write me a beautiful ode. I casually thank them, hiding a lozenge of guilt in my cheek.

An Abridged Bestiary

for Peter Kostakis

As the story goes, Noah took animals of every variety aboard his famed ark. This, however, was not the case. The aardvark and the zebra were the only animals that the concise Noah allowed to join him. "Bears to yaks be damned," he shouted, when his wife asked permission for her pet monkey to board. Not recognizing in his single-mindedness the very quality that had endeared Noah to God, she smuggled the monkey onto the ship. This feat was easily accomplished, since Noah was extremely busy the forty days that the ship labored on the swollen sea. He was revising all known bestiaries, tearing out pages and tossing them overboard with the abandon of a crazed housewife cleaning out her refrigerator. By the end of the voyage he had written what he called *Noah's Book of Animals,* a two-page pamphlet praising the grace of the aardvark and the wit of the zebra.

Contrary to popular myth, it was the stowaway monkey and not the fabled dove, who announced the sighting of land. A strong swimmer, the monkey had followed the boat, collecting the pictures that Noah discarded. On the last day of the flood, Noah saw the pictures drying on a line suspended between two palm trees in the receding water. Amazed, Noah asked God what it could mean. God admonished Noah for his frugality and blessed the intrepid monkey. The next morning all the animals were recreated, according to the discarded pictures that the monkey had saved for God.

The Sitting

"On November 8, 1875, W. C. Roentgen took a picture of his wife's hand. His mysterious rays became widely known by the mysterious letter X, but some of their significant properties became known only later. Meanwhile, enterprising photographers established 'Roentgen studios,' and did a lively business in x-ray sittings."

The line forms early each Sunday. Pregnant women bring their just-formed infants. Lovers are x-rayed in an embrace, creating a confusion of bone. One old man, wearing all black, says that he's come for a portrait of his hands folded in death. A well-dressed family waits stiffly in line. The mother adjusts her daughter's ample ears, as if they were taffy or branches of bonsai tree. Men ogle the x-ray portrait labeled with the name of a well-known courtesan. "No two are alike," says the x-ray photographer. His thin aesthetic hands hold up framed x-rays: "The men of the Academy. A dog who swallowed a key. A man milking his prize cow. The Queen Mother." Feathery shadows: even the fat lady is finely chiseled by the benevolent rays. As evening comes, the studio empties. The x-ray machine, nostalgic as a general on an empty battlefield, hums on into the night.

Toothache

I never had a toothache, but the desire to have one crossed my mind constantly. Thinking a toothache was starting, I consulted a doctor who attributed the pain to a small insect bite on the left tonsil. From that day I resolved to abandon the hope of ever feeling a quick stab of pain or a steady musical throbbing. My teeth were a fortress against invaders, the health spa of an otherwise decrepit body. Sometimes I'd see people rubbing their fingers over a spot on their cheeks hot as a sidewalk in summer. Envious, I'd fall off of chairs, steps, and bicycles, trying to land on my mouth. I took up meditation and biofeedback to focus some pain in my teeth. Like children, bored with the gifts of a visiting aunt, they remained uninvolved. Finally, quite by chance I found a way to bring myself relief. Through a new medical procedure the dentist removed one healthy tooth and implanted a large decaying molar in its place. It was worth the trouble. Now, when I pass a candystore, I buy the chewiest caramels. And when I crunch on an icecube, the pain is long and complex as a medieval tapestry.

The Woman Who Straddled the Globe

A woman straddles the globe. Her legs, like trees, become rooted in place, one foot on the North Pole, one on the South. The globe, bowing in resignation, is a sullen cowboy whose lasso is a whisper. Her voice rings out, cresting the oceans, one wave at a time. Under the woman the mountains listen to friendly advice. Each day the woman's florid spread grows new bouquets until the things around her ("sorrys," lamplight, breakfasts), the very things that lovingly called her "Roof," disappear like playing cards in the hands of Forgetfulness.

Sailing

Benjamin Franklin used to lie naked on the water, attach a kite to his leg, and let the wind carry him around the pond like a sailboat. On days when the weather was especially pleasant, you could hear him talking to himself above the jabber of various pond creatures. It was in this liquid medium that he wrote his clever epigrams. He explained that the water actually spoke to him in sentences, thus inventing the concept of "onomatopoeia."

One rainy day he met with near disaster when lightning struck the tail of his kite. The electric current traveled through his body, setting his wooden teeth aflame. For a week he lay unconscious, a Jack-o-lantern grin behind his badly blistered gums.

The Shoe and the City

A woman answers the phone every day saying "Kill me"
to the paperboy, "Kill me" to the grocer, the beautician.
A man is arrested for the offense of passivity—being
quiet in a theater. These things happen in the city where
a judge could be a glass of water. A worn-out shoe bangs
itself on a table to make a legal point. But what are they
doing in the haberdasher? Burning their coats to believe
in the after-life of their pockets? Burying their dead
under piles of shirts to rejuvenate the wretched stripes,
the fraying cuffs? And that single footprint in the park—
a gift from the road that leads to endless cafes where coffee glistens, a portrait of your own glass heart.

The Moat

Two soldiers, masquerading as trees, pass me casually on the street. Aware of the possibility that they're armed, I avert my eyes, questioning their peculiar disguise only to myself. I walk on only to come upon two trees attired as soldiers. I assume that the soldiers and the trees have made an even exchange, and aware of the possibility that the trees, as easily as the soldiers could be armed, walk directly toward my home.

Arriving there just after dark, I see that the draw-bridge has been raised. I compare my situation to that of a piece of luncheon meat destined for a sandwich, only to find that the bread it was supposed to occupy is already accounted for.

I question the possibility of swimming the narrow width of the channel. Stripping to the waist I notice how my skin catches the eerie glow of the moon, making me look terribly anemic. This hypochondriacal observation adds to my fear of attempting the swim. I empty my pockets to make the load lighter and leave their contents, some coins, a key, and a ticket stub, inside of my boot on the bank. As I submerge myself cautiously in the dark water I find that all I can think about are blue, shiny plums. Despite my mind's obsession, I find my arms and legs moving rhythmically, and remark that if they were statesmen, they would be articulate speakers.

Shivering, I lift myself out of the water and knock vigorously on the door, remembering that I've left my key in my boot on the other side of the moat. James, the butler, answers the door and acts surprised to see me partially undressed. His reaction triggers in me, for the first time this evening, the realization that I am a woman, and, for the first time in his employment with me, that he is a man. He bows graciously and offers me a dry white towel.

I question the servants unrelentingly and find that not one of them knows why the bridge was raised before I returned home. Satisfied with this answer, I settle down for the evening. My tea, hot and fragrant as ever, is brought to me and I retire to read a rather obscure book of aphorisms, comfortably wrapped in my white wool shawl, iridescent in the moonlight.

The Last Aurochs

Father wears antlers to dinner. Antlers so large that his
head resembles a small tree in winter. We no longer
look at each other but just keep eating. Mother doesn't
seem to notice it anymore. She told us to treat Father as
if nothing had happened. That was hard at first. So
much had been in the papers. It was all they talked
about in town. You see, Father destroyed the tourist
trade. In fact, he destroyed the only commerce in our
town other than cows the museum where the last
aurochs was displayed.

The last aurochs, the ancestor of our modern cow, died
in Poland in 1627. The people in that little town donated
its bones and a few artifacts to our town as a goodwill
gesture about ten years ago. Because Father fought
there in the war, they made him the curator of the
museum. There he kept the bones in a glass case, the tarnished bell on the door, and the water trough and feed
bag, always filled with cold water and the freshest alfal-
fa, in the middle of the room. Since there were no pictures of the aurochs, we had to imagine how it looked,
furrier and larger than our cows today, with sadder eyes
and a softer glance.

Father loved his job. He wouldn't have intentionally
burned down that museum if his life depended on it.
The fire started because he cared *too much*. When he'd
come home Mother would ask if he'd had a good day.
He'd always say that he had, that tourists had come, that
he'd rung the aurochs' bell for them. Nothing he said explained his drawn face and red, swollen eyes. We could
never understand his sadness until one night when we
heard some commotion in the back yard. We all ran to
the window and saw Father prancing around in the

moonlight, wearing those huge antlers. It was a beautiful dance. Father expressed the longing that the last aurochs must have felt for a companion. It was a mating dance, a dance that bulls in our country still do today. It went on until the sun came up.

Father never mentioned it to us. He'd come to breakfast looking drowsy and quietly leave for work. Soon he didn't even care about his uniform. His shirt was dirty. He lost buttons. The dance went on night after night. Soon he perfected a series of cries that went along with it. Pathetic mooing, guttural, low. Now mother looked worn too. She was worried. One night there were two aurochs out in the back yard; Father, and Mother, wearing antlers somehow implanted in her hairdo. She copied his dance but did it more demurely. She answered his calls in a voice so sweet that all of us nearly cried. In the middle of the dance, just at the point when it touched us most, something strange happened. Father screamed, "It's a lie! They aren't extinct! It's a lie!" He walked into the house and had his first sound sleep in weeks.

Father started going to work later and later. The museum suffered from his disinterest. One night a pile of old paper went up in flames. The museum burned before we could save the tarnished bell or a single bone. Since then Father doesn't speak to Mother any more. He won't take off his antlers and he won't even say the word "Cow." Sometimes I see him sending off letters. He addresses them to that town in Poland. Every day the mail comes. There is no reply. Every now and then he moos sadly, watching the tall grass swaying in the yard.

A Vegetable Emergency

There is something new among the vegetables in my garden this morning: a sinister weed, with brown, hair-like filaments. I start tugging but find it surprisingly resilient. Bracing myself like a sailor hoisting anchor in a gale, I nearly fall over backwards. The ground gives way to the head of a man, attractive, about forty, with brown wavy hair. A small white butterfly, straying from the cabbage patch, has landed above his ear. I picture Gauguin arriving in Tahiti in much the same way, a startled islander pulling him from the rhubarb-colored sand. But a head seems to be all that exists of this man. I wonder what he's doing in my garden, a city plot smaller and less enticing than even the Paradise Lounge down the street. I ask him this, but he stares off at the white fence, stony and mute.

I wonder if the head, like a hangnail, is a little discussed but nevertheless common occurrence. I consult manuals, finding only parasites, fungi, and frost among the vegetable emergencies. No mention of a head, obtrusive as a fireplug in a desert. I call up a few neighbors for advice. The are sympathetic but noncommittal.

That night I sit in bed, watching fireflies circling the jar-like head. I wonder what will happen when fall comes and I've eaten or canned all the crops. I imagine plowing up the garden, burying the head under a mound of earth, and hoping for an early blizzard. But what if the head resurfaced each year, perhaps doubled in size, edging the other vegetables far from the sunlight? One blow from my spade might dispatch it abruptly as it arrived. But what if it screamed? A head so obstinately silent, given the right situation, might be vociferous. Unable to sleep, I listen to the crickets as if to canned laughter.

Over my morning coffee, I distractedly read the newspaper. Outside the window, the head, like a silent Mafia don, dominates the garden. A sale at the greenhouse resolves the problems for me; by 9 A.M. I've purchased a dozen geranium plants. Like an expert milliner, I artfully cover the head with pink and orange flowers. Green fuzzy leaves patch closed the relentless eyes. I hang the "For Sale" sign in front of the house and wait for a prospective buyer. I hope, in its cloister of leaves, the head has vowed silence.

Fred Astaire

Ever since he danced on the ceiling in "Royal Wedding," he hasn't been the same. There is a longing, a profound blush, that starts in his toes and seizes the ankles. It is a feeling so intense that he must dash out of cabs, forgetting to tip his invisible top hat to passing ladies. Then, exhausted, he rests on a bench, feet tapping uncontrollably. Movies are impossible for Mr. Astaire to attend. No sooner is he seated than he begins to turn objects upside down: popcorn rolls down the aisle, cokes splash like buckets of dirty water. During his last interview, Mr. Astaire turned his leather chair over and proceeded to straddle its broadmost part, as if riding a buffalo. His wife smiled knowingly. His little granddaughter ran in shouting, "Grandpa, Grandpa! Pick me up!" Astaire took firm hold of the child's calves and held her like a double-handled mop, hair lightly brushing the ground. It is at moments like this that one sees an incredible transformation in Astaire's features. The deep wrinkles, engraved like monograms in fine silver, disappear. His blue eyes focus on the peak of his slanted roof and nestle there like doves.

Body and Soul

The day I drowned began like any other. I turned off the alarm clock and turned over in bed. My dreams had, once again, been of poached eggs, my usual breakfast. That morning I was in a hurry. The wind was from the east, as I had hoped. My ability to foretell its direction was strong as a bear's instinct to wake with the first whiff of spring.

The men of the village, dressed as trees and bushes to facilitate hunting, were up with the sunrise. From them I learned to wear the suit of a fish when setting sail. For years I had dragged the heavy costume down to the water's edge, marking a z-shaped pattern behind me. That day I noticed it had become frayed at the fins, in much the same ways as an old bag of flour leaks first at the seams. Struggling into the costume, the tight rubbery scales reassured me. It fit comfortably as old pajamas.

I floated far from the shore, the water sounding distant as someone else's heartbeat. Suddenly I felt a small bead of coldness, as if someone had shot me in a finger or an earlobe. This was my last memory before the fisherman caught me the next day. Elated at finding such a large fish, he carried me carefully from his boat. I felt a perverse pride that my fish outfit had been so convincing to a trained eye. While he displayed me in the marketplace, a few friends recognized my costume. To save the fisherman from humiliation, they bought me on the pretense of serving me to the village at the next religious festival. Had it been possible, I would have favored the alternative. Instead, they waited until night to peel the rubbery skin from me. They floated my costume, gleaming silver

in the moonlight, out to sea, while I, a dark stone,
watched coldly from shore.

Van Gogh's Ear

At the exhibit the ear hangs next to "Bedroom at Arles." A normal ear in every way but luminous like a flat pearl button. The lobe is the size of a thumbprint, and whiter, more pulpy than the rest of the ear. People walk past. Some gasp, some smirk, some sidle up and whisper furtively into it. One man looks awed, recreating the moment when Gauguin received it with the morning mail. The museum had to pay large sums of money to purchase the ear from its owner, a doctor in Holland, who kept it on his desk as a paperweight. This is the first public showing and the reviews have been splendid. Rubber copies of the ear are being sold at the counter. If you look closely, you can see they are exact replicas, complete to the fine red down studding the earlobe.

from

Utopia TV Store

Phantom Pain

After the leg is lost, the pain remains as an emblem; so the kidnapper cannot part with his ransom notes. The high diver, lost on the subway, flexes his muscles defensively. The crowd fades to waves in a pool eighty feet below. "There," pointing to the nose of a seated passenger, "is where I'll land." The mad bomber turns to his wife and says, "I'll give up my career for you." She pictures his delicate bombs defusing, like scenes in a home movie played backwards. Meanwhile, the kidnapper, grown careless with sentimentality, drops a ransom note on the subway seat. The train conductor, who last night dreamed of a murderer, hides the note like a stolen pistol under his cap. Later the bomber stops at a diner full of known bombers. Anxious, he drops a coffee cup, white fragments exploding at his feet.

Vanity, Wisconsin

Firemen wax their mustaches at an alarm; walls with mirrors are habitually saved. At the grocery women in line polish their shopping carts. Children too will learn that one buys meat the color of one's hair, vegetables to complement the eyes. There is no crime in Vanity, Wisconsin. Shoplifters are too proud to admit a need. Punishment, the dismemberment of a favorite snapshot, has never been practiced in modern times. The old are of no use, and once a year at their "debut," they're asked to join their reflections in Lake Lablanc. Cheerfully they dive in, vanity teaching them not to float. A visitor is not embarrassed to sparkle here or stand on his hotel balcony, taking pictures of pictures.

Evolution of the Bridge

Guaranteed in every model is a lifespan shorter than your own. The bridge of wet gardenias is designed as a study in pathos. Citizens weep past the flowery rails. Commuters are accustomed to detouring at the stringbean bridge. What could provide a better excuse for your late arrival at work? The boss, himself unable to cross the rubberband drawbridge, will praise your good sense in the matter, promote you to district manager. It is true that a foolhardy sort met his demise on the bridge of pancakes, but that is the only recorded fatality. Consider the greater good. Towns have sprung up around these passing fancies. A village thrives at the foot of a suspension bridge made of feathers. The colorful plumage draws tourists from miles around. On the green, city fathers have erected a sweet potato statue of their first mayor. At every rainfall a different citizen is sculpted into prominence. Perishable bridges have also relieved the boredom of scenery. Sunday drives are taken with a new sense of urgency. And optimism is flourishing. No longer do girders shiny as new ideas ridicule our own decline. We are treated to an ever-changing landscape as monuments are blissfully forgotten.

Subtraction

First there was addition, incestuous and pretentious.
Coupling jackals with jackals, summing sunsets and
field mice. Soon the world was packed as a third class
railway car. We tired of objects desiring us—lenses,
doorknobs, cuspidors elbowing between lovers. Scholars
developed protective philosophies, claiming they'd die
for "breathing space," but what of the common man?
His only hope was in the inventions of madmen—
evaporation chambers, metaphysical vacuums, all of
which failed. One day in a schoolroom a slow child with
glasses forgot to draw the vertical line of the plus sign
and so subtraction was born. *Minus, minus* we chanted
all day, watching our laundry recede from the clothes-
lines.

Kill Yourself with an *Objet D'Art*

Choose a heavy one, shaped like (a) your first ride in a car or (b) the Hitchcock leg-of-lamb, served at dinner to the unsuspecting detective. Or a light *objet d'art*, (c) an icecube in whose reflection is suggested the history of the subconscious.

Now choose a forehead, yours to be exact. Where your hand intersects the mirror-image forehead, strike the blow. If (a) has been your instrument, you will feel run over but sincere; if you choose (b) you will feel theatrical; (c), as you know, was the object that Freud himself surrendered to in moments of despair.

But if none of these objects appeals to you, consider the following technique: serve as executor for the will of a millionaire-idiot. He'll gladly leave you trifles and before you know, you'll be the owner of possibilities: an Ernst bed, equipped with guillotine, a Picasso woman whose lips are razorblades, a Goya with personal angels, black and familiar.

The Man Struck Twenty Times by Lightning

I've known him so long I've almost forgotten the first photo he showed me. The helpless orphan in the cloud-like bonnet abandoned in a rainstorm. And the scrapbook: "Boy Struck by Lightning on Little League Field." "Teen Struck by Lightning at Graduation Exercise." "Bride and Groom Struck by Lightning at Altar. One Dies."

Extraordinary, yes, but his relationship with lightning, which seems the most personal in nature, no longer astounds me. I sometimes think of lightning as his pushy employer. At other times *he* is the master, lightning the recalcitrant servant. He is the ship, lightning the challenging sea. His favorite is him as countryside, lightning the endless white fence.

Often I wonder whether he's contrived the danger to make his attachments more tender. I must admit I can't think of the speed of lightning without some tears. In this way I'm like the mother of the baby born with a full set of teeth. Night after night she lies awake, examining the record book, imagining its dubious future.

"Charlatan," I say on rainy nights, for he's never been struck in my presence. Yet with every weather forecast I fear his loss, knowing I'd miss those singed greetings, those thunderous goodbyes.

Rehearsal

So you want to be an orchestra. Start small. Be an instrument first. Hang eighty-eight black and white scarves out to dry on a windy day. If the neighborhood dogs circle mournfully, you are succeeding.

If you are past this step, answer the following: Can fear be your snare drum? Can your windpipe anachronize the lute? How much do your toes, those angry percussionists, respect authority?

I once knew a woman whose spine was a xylophone. Students came from miles around just to hear the exquisite "slump" into a chair. That is your competition. Can you equal it? Are you a French horn in the fetal position? Do your arms wave passionately or are they sadly reinforced against desire?

Finally you'll need to be the conductor. Try this: chew seventeen crackers into a microphone, then bow deeply. By now the audience is clapping wildly. Hum the opening bars. The seats are vibrating ever so slightly. The baton is hovering just out of reach like last night's rain.

A Definition

As a monument to beauty an artist designed a miniature windmill composed of the mustaches of the great. Though their identities have been concealed, it is rumored the work contains the mustaches of Marco Polo, Betsy Ross, Rasputin, and Galileo. The artist scrupulously grooms the windmill every morning before he takes it to the hill above town. The wind seems to favor his creation with gentle breezes and nothing is more lovely than its nonchalant curve through air. Observers often ask the artist to reveal the mustaches' origins. One tourist offered a handsome endowment difficult for a man to refuse. The response was silence. For beauty must exist without history, anonymous as boredom or glacial ice.

The Boat

I set out in a boat that is also a birdcage. Or should I say a birdcage that is somewhat a boat? For it more resembled a birdcage: light bamboo bent to meet at the peaked roof, a little swing suspended absentmindedly from the top. There *were* precedents. I'd heard of the man who went to sea in a fire engine. I imagined the waves wafting against the shiny sides, the urgent bells having nothing to ring for at sea.

How wonderful it was when the wind whistled through the rungs, setting the empty swing in motion. The water was aquamarine and the sky was always there, though I never could name its color. At first the going was perilous; the waves had never known a seaworthy birdcage, this ship without cargo or flags or sails. I instructed the birdcage to be more ship, inspiring it through tales of other vessels, the skyscraper that floated on faith alone. The bamboo seemed more formidable after that, and the sound of the boat returned to me as the sound of the sea allowing my boat to float.

I sometimes had occasion to see other boats, and I saluted politely as we passed the vacationers in pink sunglasses, the rainbow deck chairs, the bustling shuffleboard courts. I felt no jealousy for their luxury, no desire for human companionship, knowing my only companion's bamboo reflection was unique in all the ocean. As the years passed and the birdless swing rocked slowly at the peak of the ship, I knew how famous we'd be for absolutely nothing, for floating past exotic ports as the ocean wind mingled with our air.

What the Dead Eat

For centuries the dead did not eat. But new information convinces us of the dead's only tie to the living, their hunger. The concept of hunger after death shouldn't confound. Nor is it mere innuendo, whispered by those who cling to the last human pleasure like an old coat sleeve. For the dead will tell you that their insatiability is no cause for hope. Let me make matters simple. For those who look forward to death as a final rest, expect a canceled vacation. Even the most pious have turned down heaven for a greasy leg of mutton. Mothers do not hear the sobs of their children. Eulogies are delivered to empty picture frames. For all the dead see are gleaming platters of rolls and fragrant cheeses. It is told that a certain world leader missed a pot roast so sorely that God in pity granted him a final bite. That is the only way the dead are allowed to eat. Do not expect this favor. Societies have always understood the ritual importance of the condemned's last meal, but not until now has its futility been realized. For the hunger of the dead is life's revenge and it implicates even the soul; many have pined away for a crust so light, a meringue so airy they could inspire flight. As a whim a few gluttons and mystics have been excused from the "Great Hunger," a term favored by the dead over the more proper "Reverse Transubstantiation." They rest oblivious as tables. Others, in false hope, take their plates to the grave or go out in an orgy of etiquette, napkins tucked neatly under chins, salad forks poised in rigor mortis. But authorities admonish. Do not ask what the dead eat. It is too tragic.

The Meaning of Anxiety

Can you ever look at yourself again without wanting to swallow a cash register? Try to relax. List the potential murders, the disappearances. See the globe become a blue balloon held by a schoolboy.

Remember the past for reassurance, the lesson in perspective, for instance. How the man in fedora receded endlessly down the railroad tracks only to re-appear in next year's arithmetic book, page 248. Recall the happy hours spent peekabooing with nothingness in that urinous pink and white year of your birth.

When feeling low compare your life to that of others less fortunate than yourself. Consider the maker of dolls' voices— lying in bed all day inventing doll dialects, doll monologues, doll witticisms. The occupational hazard, a bone in the ear chronically vibrating like a tuba in a corner of a warehouse. You'd long for a spring in which deafness is a garden dreamed in slow motion.

But you've never understood how another's misery can lighten your own. Don't they exist side by side like cars at a stoplight? Lately yours has become so compelling. A sigh that forms like an icicle. A religion of swallowing. A system of visions and hallucinations widely accepted as currency. And the fatal proof of that condition. Sudden-ly the mundane appears fearfully beautiful. Your shaky laundry must be folded delicately as spiderwebs. Your hair grows musically. You yearn to meet others with the same blood type.

Bees in one's bonnet is how it's often described, but today no euphemism will suffice. Outside your window birds fly single file, carrying the primary colors of your former life.

Utopia TV Store

Amid rows of TVs, screens blank as postcards from
cemeteries, we lose ourselves. And while we wait to have
our sets repaired, we discuss the owner's inventions: a
shadow that never changes length or width, a test pattern of pure memory adapting through the ages of man.

Who says there are no heroes? We love the way he
plunges his hand into sets, no regard for personal safety.
It's those explosions no more frightening than weather
reports from other cities that calm us.

Often customers who die leave their TVs in his care, he's
told us with some tenderness. "Here's one that a widow
left behind ten years ago. Watching it's like washing
clothes underwater. Total immersion. And let me tell
you. It's better off than any of us. Inherited a Cadillac
Seville, a houseboat, an empty lot. But does it need
those things? Examine its console. Dark, smooth. Look
at the antenna. No rigidity there, relaxed, wanting nothing."

"Of course it's happy here," we add, taking our usual
cue. Yes, Utopia TV Store is always open. Even on
Christmas Eve we're treated as guests. Mistletoe decking
the sets. Perry Como beaming in on every capable tube
as we focus our eyes on a pinpoint. Automatically tuning
in and fading out, we listen to the steady CLICK CLICK,
knowing we owe it our lives, more hazy and blurred
with each day.

Anonymous Thoughts from Home

Sometimes I feel as though I'm walking backwards or live in a forgotten age. After all, aren't we rickety chairs, rattling to prove our worth? And yet in living we can be generous and think a vital thought.

At least that's what I thought. Once on a train going backwards, I met a man too generous for his own good. To flatter me, he asked my age, and I, to prove him foolish, said, "Sir, I am a chair."

An idea, too, is part of a design, the chair on which I sit abstracted. Had I thought myself a genius, trying to prove that one could live a life viewed backwards? No, this is not a comforting age when it is facile to be generous.

Coleridge was not a generous man. In fact, he never offered a chair to visitors, even of an advanced age. Still I think of his phrase "toy of thought" with veneration. "Thought of toy" is the same phrase backwards. (What does that prove?)

Giving gifts may not prove you generous. A socially backward person might give a blind man a camera. Did you ever offer a chair to a friend who couldn't sit? I must admit it entered my thought. Try, if you have the inclination, to give a sportscar to a mummy despite its age.

When is it said that a philosophy comes of age?
Do primary colors always prove true to their nature?
Can an animal think an unoriginal thought?
Would it be called generous to offer a stranger your child?
Who invented the reclining chair?

47

Will the best man win even if he can only walk backwards?

If I could travel backwards to a kinder age, I'd buy a comfortable chair, a document to prove that people once were generous, at least that's what they thought.

In the Hospital

I'm in the hospital to have a baby. My two roommates
are a porpoise and a tiny Oriental woman. The nurses
are oblivious to us. One has put at least ten coats of pink
polish on her hideously sharp nails. I'm still able to walk
around, and because I seem in better shape than my two
roommates, I find myself assuming the nurse's duties.
Every fifteen minutes I must submerge the porpoise's
head in a large bowl of water so that she may breathe.
When I lift her, her body feels clammy and strange
against my white hospital gown. The Oriental woman is
on the delivery table, legs in stirrups. When I look up
her to see if the baby is about to be born, I am able to
view all of her vital organs in textbook color. Finally I
get so aggravated from lack of assistance that I hit the
nurse with the porpoise's tail. She keeps polishing her
nails.

from

New Faces of 1952

Lost and Found

I am looking for the photo that would make all the difference in my life. It's very small and subject to fits of
amnesia, turning up in poker hands, grocery carts,
under the unturned stone. The photo shows me at the
lost and found looking for an earlier photo, the one that
would have made all the difference then. My past evades
me like a politician. Wielding a fly-swatter, it destroys
my collection of cereal boxes, my childhood lived close
to the breakfast table. Only that photo can help me lo-
cate my fourteen lost children, who look just like me.
When I call the Bureau of Missing Persons, they say,
"Try the Bureau of Missing Photos." They have a fine collection. Here's one of Calvin Coolidge's seventh wedding.
Here's one of a man going over a cliff on a dogsled.
Here's my Uncle Arthur the night he bought a peacock.
O photo! End your tour of the world in a hot air balloon.
Resign your job at the mirror-testing laboratory. Come
home to me, you little fool, before I find I can live
without you.

You remember *New Faces of 1952*, entertainers blurred and green as bad counterfeit. From her lap you watched your mother watch TV. Sometimes she'd accompany the aquamarine vocalist in "Sentimental Journey," but always during commercials she looked confused. Was she trying to separate your squalling from your future as critics detach art from art? The dominant hue was infant red. Face it. Your childhood was shaped by daily viewing of *Divorce Court*. To enhance your witness box approach to life, you began each sentence with "Your Honor" and practiced crying in a full-length mirror. As credits cascaded down the screen, you admired the boomers and gaffers, unheralded as bacteria. By now your tears had a charisma so strong they performed without you at Edsel sales. With the crisp, high step of majorettes, they preceded you down Main Street. When your mother questioned, you pleaded the Fifth or practiced evasion: "Inventing the enemy," you said in the mirror. An optimist, she labelled you artistic. The other choice was worse.

Tenderitis

I want to tell jokes
about tie salesmen and girls
named Dolores, whose letters
are always in French,
always the subjunctive mood.
Sadder than diamonds
that would spell your name,
you, whom the Indians called
Dies of Heartfelt Laughter.
Killing in a strange orange light,
muted as bees and humble.
The hum of blue weather
announces my proper angle,
and I am numb and kneeling
at the Shrine of Holy Women
Ironing Shirts. I, meaning you,
is a gesture, like a runaway
milkhorse, restless in ghost form.
I ask for the dumbness of tradition,
steering me toward a sideways reckoning,
an imperative satisfaction.
Please, when localities fail,
and the underbrush is lit
by false candles, tell me
what to do with history
that fashioned you at my feet.

Spring

Mrs. Smith takes Mr. Smith in the closet while the
children dream in unison of Napoleon. It happens every
spring. Spirit pounds flesh, and you think the newsman
said "languor." Next door the professor is vibrantly
thinking, theories brightening the room at nine P.M. *So,*
he sighs, *in this instance the British spelling is correct.* A
fruit fly circles over his dictionary. Another battle won.
In the nearby church a bell insists in the highest tower.
It reminds us of a toothache or nostalgia. Meanwhile,
she's ripped her nylons on his limitations. He wears
suspenders, the nerve! You close your eyes and point to
a map, finding yourself in an Amazon so blue you worry
for the ocean. That's the give and take of it, the getting
out of yourself at least for a stroll down the Avenue of
Busted Cups. It's March 19th, time to slaughter the poin-
settia. A white milk oozes from the stem onto the
mahogany. The kind is dead. If your ideas had form like
a milk bottle left on the porch, you'd take them in the
closet and caress them. You wouldn't be discreet. You'd
understand the implications but finally wouldn't care.
After all, this is a poem about love.

Obbligato for My 29th Birthday

A *libeccio* blows open
the southwest, Italian curtain.
A lovely word, found on my husband's desk.
A trespasser there, I'm poaching it
here and now. Such opportunities abound:
You can stow away on a tramp steamer
swarming with linguists and share your bunk
with the greasy, spectacled man whose treatise
is "The Derivation of *Frambesia*."
Or collect etymology in the way
my brother does beer cans.
Better yet, buy a tape recorder,
placc it under your pillow and play dead.
By morning you'll be juggling words
like a Keystone Cop. Please world,
no kibosh today. Allow me
my tootle, my xyster, my *libeccio*.

Breasts

If I were French, I'd write
about breasts, structuralist treatments
of breasts, deconstructionist breasts,
Gertrude Stein's breasts in Père-Lachaise
under stately marble. Film noire breasts
no larger than olives, Edith Piaf's breasts
shadowed under a song, mad breasts raving
in the bird market on Sunday.
Tanguy breasts softening the landscape,
the politics of nipples (we're all equal).
A friend remembers nursing,
his twin a menacing blur. But wait,
we're in America, where breasts
were pointy until 1968. I once invented
a Busby Berkeley musical with naked women
underwater sitting at a counter
where David Bowie soda-jerked them
ice cream glaciers. It sounds so sexual
but had a Platonic airbrushed air.
Beckett calls them dugs, which makes me think
of potatoes, but who calls breasts potatoes?
Bolshoi dancers strap down their breasts
while practicing at the bar.
You guess they're thinking of sailing,
but probably it's bread, dinner,
and the *Igor Zlotik Show* (their
Phil Donahue). There's a photo of me
getting dressed where I'm surprised
by Paul and try to hide my breasts, and another
this year, posed on a pier, with my breasts
reflected in silver sunglasses. I blame
it on summer when flowers overcome gardens
and breasts point at the stars. Cats
have eight of them, and Colette tells

of a cat nursing its young while
being nursed by its mother. Imagine the scene
rendered human. And then there's the Russian
story about the woman...but wait,
they've turned the lights down, and Humphrey
Bogart is staring at Lauren Bacall's breasts
as if they might start speaking.

Jails burst with pride
and milk was the first to spill
from the frugal apothecaries.
The blindfolded cowboys
smelled of card games
and saloon girls' eyes
were steep and collapsible
dreaming of Paris.
For dinner there was
pickled breast of sky
and later robins in every pot.
The one-armed hero had a cloud
to rest his head on.
Often he sleepily muttered,
"The map is ample. Bring me
my medals, Louise."
Postcards were invented then
and so: musicians on sailboats
played rhapsodies, patients
took strolls to Europe and back,
no one got dirty.
In all of this the weather
cooperated and sayings
of the avenue were displayed
in public places:
Fatigue deserves a paycheck.
Dancing girls have no notion
of continuity. Never give a major
a bouquet of remedies.
Sometimes this touched us
collectively. And we said,
"It is good to be part of this
salient breeze, this necklace
we wear only gradually."

Identity Principle

Triplets are so embarrassing, too much soup in the soup of life. Who needs an alphabet with three O's, a tangled birth, a troika of woes? Picture the mother, swelled as a cloud, the gallop of three heartbeats like a posse through her. Or twins, those clever monkeys, allowed to eat at table. Identical birthmarks, matching hairnets, the sound and the echo. And old age: one twin wheels the other before him, meeting himself after the stroke. So you decide, even among brothers and sisters raucous as wedding guests, to be an only child. The stance you take in making love, in walking crookedly, in robbing the sperm bank. Until you have a child and people say, "She looks just like you!" In her face you see the same wish to be an island so distant she'll never see another pleasure boat.

A Name

Suppose your parents had called you Dirk. Wouldn't
that be motive enough to commit a heinous crime, just
as Judys always become nurses and Brads, florists?
After the act, your mom would say, "He was always a
good boy. Once on my birthday he gave me one of those
roses stuck in a glass ball. You know, the kind that never
gets soggy"— her Exhibit A. Exhibit B: a surprised
corpse, sharing a last moment of Dirk with the mortician. And Dad would say, "Dirk once won a contest by
spelling the word 'pyrrhic,'" and in his alcohol dream he
sees the infant Dirk, all pink and tinsel, signing his birth
certificate with a knife. Still, Dirk should have known
better. He could tell you that antimony is Panama's
most important product. He remembered Vasco da
Gama and wished him well. Once he'd made a diorama
of the all-American boyhood: a little farm, cows the size
of nails, cottonball sheep, a corncob silo, but when he
signed it Dirk, the crops were blighted by bad faith. Too
bad. And don't forget Exhibits C, D, E . . . The stolen
eclair, the zoo caper, the taunting of a certain Miss W.,
who smelled of fried onions. It was his parents' fault.
They called him Dirk.

Sotto Voce

Although she's only four, my daughter knows Spanish.
Say *blanco*, she demands, say *negro*. Words are the
finest toys, she tells me with eyes that are arrows. My
husband speaks with the virtuosity of a drummer:
suspiration, humidor, revivify. Beautiful words float up-
wards like jets sewing clouds. If my cat could only
speak, it would be in a shrill nasal French I wouldn't understand. Languages wash over me, scratched in cold
telephone booths, tapped on windowpanes. I am sorry
to admit that I'm inventing yet another, in the dark, furtively as one remembers an obscene old kiss. Just as I
am thinking about it, my daughter shouts *verde, verde*.
She thinks so much depends on it— palm trees, parsley,
dollar bills— that I can't disappoint her. Foolish girl, I
think, locking up my new language. Then *verde* dissol-
ves, naked and bloodless, into the busy air.

Some Noise

A room that looks out on the sea
that is cardboard and paint.
The natives dive for postcards
and Bob Hope walks on water.
The bellboy assures you
by a peculiar tilt of his head
that he is deaf. You've landed
with your lemons, lists and doubts
all real as candy but would stay
if asked, dreaming a harbor
and a man in jodhpurs, probably
Rudyard Kipling, who shows you
how to dance a measured,
proper waltz. Monocled and
amused, he is happy
you are visiting his century
with your practical wisdom.
With a studious attention
to possibility you tell him
that sleep is a harvest ripped open,
a sign beating Thursday,
sudden wanting hard as paint,
invisible advice that feathers
you home, racehorses tunneling
to China along an axis of pure feeling,
the Pisan wind sweeping toasters,
mixers, anachronisms before it,
voices to swarm, a focus to capture,
teeth to bite the time in half.
He nods. Suddenly it's morning
with its hooded colors,
its unforgiving Alps,
its sensory tips,
blue and rude as soap.

Frankly

I have a notion the skyline is false,
a rude set of gangster mugs of the century.
Sixteen years to go and counting, we'll call ours
the age of being succinct, represented by empty
quotation marks etched on our Aubrey Beardsley
mood-generators. In China a philosopher once
called his age, "Time of Ship Fallen into the Sea."
Ours won't be the age of Yul Brynner or of the dentist
whose plastic heart we've already forgotten.
I want to be around New Year's Eve, 1999, gray hair
and streamers, and proclaim like a Russian poet,
"Thank God it's over!" New century arriving
with its coffee can of pennies, immigrant worker
whose father hopes for the best. We want
the best too, poor old century, waning moon,
small sculpture in the shape of the genius' head.
We want shiny new life and permission to close
a slippery chapter of imprecision we'll call
"Falling Headfirst on Memory's Pier."

The Color Red

F.D.R. died before I was born, defining my historical context: it's like life after Lincoln, in the administration of Chester Alan Arthur. In a newsreel I recently saw, Roosevelt is seated in a miniature velvet chair, small-talking with Sissie, a niece, a daughter or a grandchild. *What's our campaign slogan,* he asks, face blooming for the camera. *Happy days are here again,* she pronounces, her elegant little voice the size of a smear. The same reel notes that the Queen (Elizabeth's mother, I mentally adjust) ate her first hot dog at the White House. My mother's senior class photo dates from that era. It reveals a dramatic widow's peak and lipstick applied well over the lipline. Of course the photo is black and white, so her lips appear so obscenely dark that she might have been a graduating vampire. When I was small she had a favorite red halter top with a built- in bra. Her breasts pointed like stars, my first memory of color. Still I can't help feeling nostalgic for black and white, those old newsreels that moved so quickly that speech was more gesture than language.

Family legend has it that my great-grandmother, Ida, was the first Jewish woman in Bialystok, Russia, to wear lipstick. A shame on her family, she also smoked cigarettes though her husband Herschel, a little monkey of a man, disapproved. He concentrated on culture, teaching the neighborhood boys violin. He is said to have played so beautifully he might have been a concert performer were he not Jewish. I imagine an organ grinder's monkey dressed in a miniature tuxedo, first violin in the Minsk symphony. No documentation exists of my great- grandmother's habits. The only photo of her, a cracked sepia, shows a shriveled woman of seventy in a hooded secular robe. In another life she might have been an abbess or an austere tree. My great-grandmother's family left Russia because her son, with hair the color of yams, was caught stealing apples from a Christian landowner's orchard. Neighbors warned of his impending arrest. Their last view of Russia was by night train, of a region darker than they'd ever suspected they lived in, a night with no moon or one so small it was too disappointing to notice. In America Herschel went into wholesale fruit. The photo shows a tame animal pawing a triangle of apples. If there were justice, the son who had hastened their departure wouldn't have become a real estate baron in Los Angeles, shooting eighty at the Buena Vista Golf Club, *For Members Only*. Like so many boys my great-grandfather taught violin, he would have stayed in black and white, dying on newsreel, a stain on a wheatfield, the revolution.

Mamie Eisenhower always wore bright red hats and bobbed her head. I used to think she was related to Mrs. Neilson down the street, whose husband died by falling off the roof he was shingling with green tiles. Mrs. Neilson had the same cocker spaniel bangs as Mamie Eisenhower. She also bobbed her head. Because she was an alcoholic, my mother believed. Maybe she shouted up to her husband that lunch was ready the moment before he fell. Signalling he'd be down, he lost hold. But that wasn't the sequence. When Mrs. Neilson came home from shopping, she found him lying in the gangway, floursack white, neck broken. I think she always bobbed her head to recapitulate the fall.

Twice I've been stung by wasps. I was only three the first time, the day of my grandfather's funeral. When my mother told me that he was dead, I went running into my grandparents' room. Dead meant lying down, so he'd be in bed. My grandmother had been mending an apron, still trapped in her sewing machine like a heap of animal, the only life in the room. On the black vinyl seat of the funeral hearse, my forearm harassed a wasp. A red lump the size of an adult elbow grew under the skin,

my second memory of color. Twenty years later I drove
cross-country with Paul in a maroon Chrysler Fury.
Lying on his lap I watched the sky change from Illinois
to Indiana to Ohio to West Virginia. Red needlemarks
on the map named towns like Frigid and Tater. *Let's
cover our eyes, choose one to die in and drive,* I told him.
Closing my eyes to laugh with him, I felt the record of
the event, a single tooth in my back, the wasp.

Adjectives

Her sprained blue
waffle-print pajamas
on the red red red
green bed. The
nauseating rain,
the ancient stairs.
My blouse is dripping
in the ancient rain
on Rhodes, the castle
of St. John of the Cross
restored by Mussolini.
In the photo you can
sense an airy calm.
Call it reticent
to swallow words
that swallow them-
selves: Elderberries,
flashlights, horse-
shoe crabs and lime-
stone provide a hazy
cotton imperfection
to the day as it's
remembered. I'll carve
in stone the friendly
sky and asterisk for
clarity. The way it's
written stays. The tinny
world that never glows
without us shining in it.

March

If your name began with X,
I'd call it pleasure to describe
the Alpha Constellation
chained and glowing
like a radium night stick
you brought home to satisfy
your longing for pure danger.
Cast-iron defeat is second
only to earlobes on the day
of reckoning blue sky.
A bicycle's blur perfumed
to last forever. Permission
for seizures not granted
but swallowed whole and beating.
The world is blue and obvious
as your throaty scorn
when alien sense is null
and leaning into light.
The dancers have arrived
to spackle us with angles,
meaning French is the beginning
of the breath that clings
to cliffs as you sail home.
I believe you in this air
that sets my hair on end.
Let's go to the sacred island
that's always closed for repairs
so always poignant in the abstract
like a festival in Norway.
Then announce our coming
to the open window
that sets our fever squarely,
loose or shallow as a statue,
smiling with closed eyes.

Miss Congeniality

Even as an embryo, she made room for "the other guy."
Slick and bloody, she emerged quietly: Why spoil the
doctor's best moment? When Dad ran over her tricycle,
she smiled, and when Mom drowned her kittens, she
curtsied, a Swiss statuette. Her teachers liked the way
she sat at her desk, composed as yesterday's news. In
high school she decorated her locker with heart-shaped
doilies and only went so far, a cartoon kiss at the door.
She read the classics, *The Glamorous Dolly Madison*, and
dreamed of marrying the boy in the choir whose voice
never changed. Wedding photos reveal a waterfall where
her face should be. Her husband admired how she
bound her feet to buff the linoleum. When she got old,
she remembered to say pardon to the children she no
longer recognized, smiling sons and daughters who sat
at her bedside watching her fade to a wink.

Hairdo

Part avalanche, part retort, it begins inside the unknowing scalp. Pay attention to the symptoms. No matter how even the part, how tight the bun, a hairdo may take residence. Squatters' rights exist beyond the law: try arresting a hairdo. The compelling insistence of the hairdo to a life of its own (witness its growth after death) rivals the legendary tenacity of gold prospectors. The day it is born the will collapses; the mind embraces the change like a convert the picture of his prophet.

It is Tuesday. And the fern that is her hairdo has grown overnight. First she is logical— what did she eat for dinner? what dream? The comb is useless and so is the scarf. So she boards the usual bus for work, beaming randomly at the passengers, thankful for their discretion. Not only do they ignore *her* fern but the nun with the shopping bag bangs and the driver with the broccoli coif (strange she never noticed them before). Or is it that only she can detect the change, as the adolescent girl in her dark bedroom touches her breasts, growing like radishes under the skin?

Learning To Listen

When I was eight years old, I got the measles. For two weeks, my parents like to recall, I was sick as sin, sick as a dog, sick as a scurvied sailor. My fever over 103, I lay in bed remembering odd parcels of language: "Children should be seen and not spoil the soup." "Phil, fix the helicopter so it won't snow on our layer cake." Sleep offered no relief. My mind spun with mythological halfbreeds, dachshunds welded to Airedales, my friend Ginny joined at the waist to a telephone pole. Trying to describe my visions to my worried parents, I was offered a camphored washcloth.

After a week of semi-consciousness, I came around. Smelling like a new person, I sat up in bed and demanded entertainment. Since my eyes were still light-sensitive, my mother suggested I listen to records I'd never heard, ballads about golf, Coney Island, and kreplach, containing bawdy metaphors I didn't understand. I had been so ill that time was no longer a continuum of experience. Listening to Lenny and the Jewish Rednecks *was* my childhood. Even after the illness passed and the records were stashed, whenever my mother spoke I still heard, "Parsnip, if you don't take out the zero factor, you won't get your declension this week."

Oh

In the demo ammo
Valentino night wc hauled
projectors to this shore.
Our passports were a stamp
of Octavio in Borneo
riding atop Flavio. O,
the sky was filled with sky
and the names formed
on the beach when we arrived.
You called it home,
a tensile moment balanced
on your palm like time
stalled in a ballerina
made of plastic, painted
skirt that billows red.
Who's to say she's small
and unnecessary?
That the storm, slowly
ripping the coast
on the map he holds,
cannot illustrate terror?
Take back your logic,
your camel's hump of reason.
The underworld is green
and welcoming. It's a secret
we don't speak except
in spring when breath will
shrug like shoulders
that we love. I'd grasp
the singing at the window.
No signs issue to explain
what we're to touch. Together,
we know some truths that merge

our mouths with curves
that some call beauty.

Speedreading Homer

Suppose the past is an empty library,
the present, a dreamy boathouse,
the future, you name it.
Suppose you had all your life
to find the right word, no list
of obligations long as a ladder
to oblivion. What would you do?
Lie down in your best dress
for a century snooze, outstrip
Rip Van Winkle with your interest
in nothing? Suppose life paid you
no compliments and thank you
was an expletive. Would you commit
to memory Alexander's singed books,
speedread Homer, then on to particle
physics? I asked a panel of experts
what they would do with an extra life,
awarded casually as a slice of pie
from your mother's windowsill. They
agreed on the need for salt in the diet
and the cool blush of impatience.

How We Went

It used to be we'd die of grippe, malodorous breath, or
by a curse. Death was generic, like the peas I bought
yesterday, smaller, but, yes, pea-green. Some by an over-
sight, the heart an erratic drummer, or by an obsession,
a thought ice-fast in brain. Observed without explana-
tion: the sinking of a steeple through an attic window,
the sudden dimming of one's shoes, a slackening of
hatred for a friend. Suppose a man said goodnight to his
wife and by some sign she knew: a kettle belched, a cat
arched under a chair, or her own breath caught, a faulty
clock hand.

Machinery

1

I didn't understand the term *deus ex machina* until I thought back to Sunday drives down dim Chicago streets. We'd pass the Cracker Jack factory with its giant Cracker Jack box propped on the lawn. Dad wouldn't slow down, even though I asked that my snapshot be taken on the site. No time to stop: We were heading for Midway Airport to watch the planes take off. My sister and I would stop fighting; even Bubi, deaf and beyond human suffering, saluted the *fliegen Machinen* in her pidgin Yiddish. Our 1957 Chevy was silver with a red stripe for one reason: to emulate its skyworthy brother.

2

I always imagined the father in *The Glass Menagerie* leaving home on an airplane. If my father had ever done the same, he'd have left on a stout propeller plane bound for …I never knew.

He never did. Instead he chose the airport every Sunday because other locations had been eliminated. In a forest preserve, for instance, we once had seen a nude man sitting on a park bench. His pose was calm and alert, as if he were waiting for us to arrive.

Once a woman accused Bubi of stealing a gray cardigan sweater three sizes too small for her, left momentarily on a bench in the Jackson Park Rose Garden. Bubi denied it fiercely in Yiddish, my embarrassed mother translating into English. Now we'll all go to jail, I thought, ready for tears. Dad was silent, chanting "Airport, airport," which is where we drove every Sunday after that. A few weeks later, under a bulging pillow in Bubi's bedroom, I saw a limp sleeve plastered to the sheets, a certain gray cardigan.

3

Or maybe it was part of a system. My father was an accountant and had a weekly ledger. Under CREDITS he could have written, "A peaceful trip to the airport, five planes sighted." DEBITS: "Bubi in front, Delia in back with the kids." I would ask my father to see the ledger, but he died five years ago and not in an airplane. In a new Chevy Malibu the color of cauliflower, a good piece of machinery. He called everything propelled by energy machinery: cars, tricycles, lawn mowers, electric shavers, pencil sharpeners, and, of course, airplanes.

Machinery, after all, had brought us to Chicago. My grandfather sailed from Austria to evade service in World War One, learned English and became a barber on the Santa Fe Railroad, Chicago to Los Angeles. When Aunt Molly was a child, he cut Clark Gable's hair and sent her a few locks, which she kept framed in her kitchen. When I was a teenager, he cut Sergio Franchi's hair and saved me a curl. When he presented it, I asked, "Who's Sergio Franchi?" Once a year Grandfather took an airplane in from Los Angeles to visit us, and when he died they sent him home in a silver casket. My father went alone to meet him at the airport.

4

My mother mistrusts machinery. Bubi always sat in front on drives in case of a serious accident. I didn't perversely assume this later in life. It was a given of childhood, like the name of an elderly neighbor. Whenever my mother flies, she takes out flight insurance with an ironic gleam in her eye. If you buy a policy, the plane won't crash. Slip up once, you're a goner. Once an engine went out on her jet. All it meant was an unscheduled landing in Reno, and then a second steak dinner served on the new plane, complimentary drinks, extra bottles of Scotch. She owes it to her insurance.

<h2 style="text-align:center">5</h2>

My youngest son was almost born on an airplane. I flew to New York during my eighth month, defying airline rules. Alex is a cautious child, afraid of the monkeybars, near-sighted as an old beggar. My daughter is partial to trains. They are sensible. I can imagine the good-byes I'll share with them when they're older. Off to college, on skiing trips, to visit friends, we'll carry on as I used to at airports, kissing as if it meant forever. Airports are the perfect climate for sentiment. I used to imagine that if my parents ever separated, they'd reconcile at gate 19.

Casablanca is the story of my parents' secret life. My mother stays with Father after all, although he's put her life in danger. She won't take that airplane without him. One morning my father said, "See you later" to my mother, walked out the door, and was dead two hours later.

If I have another child, she'll be born on an airplane. I've heard that children born in supermarkets receive free groceries, and children born in department stores, the finest layettes. In certain religions, children born in church enjoy a ritual significance in the community. No greater honor could come to a child of the 20th century than to arrive in a 747, 39,000 feet above the earth.

<h2 style="text-align:center">6</h2>

The first time I took an airplane alone I was fourteen and visiting my sister in Baltimore. After the tearful good-bye, I sat next to a sailor named Vince. He was

twenty-three and going home on leave. He bought me
two whiskey sours, patted me on the wrist, and said he
liked my poodle-curled spring coat. My sister and her
husband met me on schedule, and Vince turned the
corner past Avis forever. Six years later I took a plane
West after saying good-bye to a lover. Pressing Mother's
philosophy, I closed my eyes and dared the plane to fall.
"Where are we?" I asked my seatmate, eyes closed for a
count of 2,000. "In the sky!" he replied unequivocally.

7

Every summer the Blue Angels burst across the sky.
Cars on the Outer Drive stop in mid-lane to stare. I think
of war.

8

After our Sunday drives we'd test more machinery. At a
grill where hamburgers arrived in a miniature train on
silver tracks, I'd await my burger with the exhilaration
that my father saved for planes. Living at home over
summers in college, I'd come in late at night. My mother
was always asleep. My father, engrossed in an old war
movie, seemed transported. When I spoke to him, he'd
look past me.

"Do you like the movie?"

He didn't reply.

"Do you know what I saw last night? I saw *Casablanca*."

Only now, in my own fits of inattention, do I realize that
he wasn't listening. Sometimes when my children ask
me questions, I look out the window over their heads,
trying to imagine what my father was seeing.

Liarium

Some day an element will be found
that will explain the obvious.
We will be clear in small doses.
Scientists will call it Liarium,
and its contents will break
the heart: the bum who wants
two more cents to pay his tax
on coffee. The look that steals
as it gives relief. Coffee beans
that have come all the way from
the Amazon. Yellow tulips, dying
in their waterless vase, where
someone put them out of eagerness.
Without them I am nothing as fire
is nothing in a desert. End of
apostrophe. All is hesitation
blinking before the ancient
question: Are they possible,
like good and bad in Dickens?
Like sardines in the cold black
seas of Norway? Like Ethiopian
piano tuners? Like glass tables?
I see myself as language spilled
on the floor, mementos of my
brave past efforts: "Ode to
Whistling," "Ode to Harry
Belafonte," "Ode to Curls," "Ode
to White Asparagus." I am certain
I am only evidence, poor music,
self-diagnosed apologies
mumbled in the empty foyer
after the matinee has ended.

The Song

Clarity of insistence
gauche or gone
radiates a corner
sliced whole and small.
A voice sails bluely
on a lilypad of grease.
We find it touching
to discern the mechanism
of delight or twist
an eyelash compass hand
slowly until a cause issues,
a result is stymied,
never lived but full
of information.
An assurance longer
than breath, a beautiful
old corner cut in bone.
We want to feel it fettered
or distracted, not nodding
in traditional lace, light
a partner we expected
but found violent.
If you knew the edge
of what we crossed,
you would have admired
our blank inventions.
Let them pass for what
is Latin, the reverse
of plains and real mountains
ground of glass we touched
in our arriving,
abrasive ending to the notes.

Birthday Poem

For Paul

Your pale regiment
is not usual as style
or tours of Peru.
A pin-striped siren,
a handy silhouette
to place on England's
edge. Like green,
like stone, like partial
resignation on Endurance
Street, home of three
saints. Overserious
and breathing, taxed
to the limit of decorum
with a gradual pride
that's engraveable.
The door to mechanics,
a science of light bulbs
that rattle like marimbas.
"Paolo, the beautiful"
pinnacle explaining
treason at two in the
morning. Tell me a
grim lullaby we can't
sleep to, worthy
of machines that under-
stand Henry James.
This delicate living
excites me. As the
dash is my witness,
unsure of itself in
its deep attachment
to your nautical humor,
oaths and compasses.

Tragedy on Ice

You were naturalized in May
when a burst of Aaron Copeland
set your wisteria blooming.
Your plate of whatever it was
cooled on the porch
near the billboard cowboy.
The Robinson Crusoe guilt-tremor
passed, leaving you grown and abstract
as jokes about corn.
You had your expectations
and it was indeed depressing
when Anna Karenina proved
she couldn't skate just when
you hoped she'd fall
to her usual death.
Now the skater's a bird
in "Peter and the Wolf,"
and the kids are cheering; cheered,
she flies away. You have to
grow up somewhere, so why not
in the poem? You'll make it
part of your better past,
constructed of soup cans
and rocky pinnacles serving
when memory fails.
Of real heroism (stage variety)
you know only this:
the tenor weighs more
than a desk filled with phone-
books, the diva's a mother-
in-law, but a floodlight
illumines his hair that shines
like tin and she flashes a note
that will save us all in the end.

Chuckling asides aside,
we'll call it beauty. The skaters
keep thwacking the ice
with letters you once mailed
then forgot because nothing
really happened but did
in Virginia where you never were.
Baroque periwigs illustrate
a virtue you understand
but cannot share, making the ice
the protagonist. The damp pants,
gate swinging outward, Prokofiev
shuffle introduce a pale nightmare
figure-eighting over the edge
of the pool you wanted there
for the sake of the obvious.

The Sheik of Araby

I could almost touch you
as you faded into art
down the silky conduit
I designed in Venice
late that summer, no,
that fall. I love you
with a distraction
marked by dancing.
Our snub-nosed cortege
needed no flowers.
It was our melody
we tossed from cliffs.
Romance traveled
epistemologically slow,
asking inches.
Our blue tradition
needed no curator.
In our Napoleonic exile
we read our lines
in the vanishing afternoons.
The desert caravans
were jazzy. Their sheet music
blew away and we drove on,
one wingspan at a time.
Now we are anyone's.
You nod. I whistle.
The pathos of celluloid
wrapped us whole.

A Theory of Tears

Weddings won't make you cry
though I'll cry for you, mean
madonna, police chase through
the park, beautiful arms of
sleepers. I'll cry for the whole
upstairs, the empty bar, and for
the parade that's caught fire
in front of the Chinese ambassador.
I'll cry for the case of nerves
that fills the nun's room when she
curses her fate: to be among school-
children who never change their
clothes. Maybe I'll conjure a patron
saint of frustration and place him
at the bingo parlor with a losing
card holding his breath until he's
passed out. (Call him Saint Swoon.)
Agility is what you need to use
the ivory bridge of your escape,
the Saturnian slant of spring.
Shake your glorious head or lose
your way, a bulldozer with mixed
emotions. Yesterday cracked open
like a letter that promised your
death. Monosyllabic, the weather
hasn't prepared you. Pieces of light
grow thin and disappear. No tears.
Good night, blank lips that part
when breathing. The violinist's
trousseau of black gowns floats
on the water of your grudging dreams.

Poem for Ted

(1934-1983)

I'm writing this in verse for you
as Sox are tied at zero, weather gray,
and Koren hates ballet, where mean kids

dance alone. Cheer enters, clumsily,
stage left, when Kenward sends a card
from Weeki Wachi, hokey Florida,

bubbling aquamarine swimmer with an S.O.S.
hello. I wonder if my "this and that" routine
will count. I've always doubted my allure

but maybe what's around me is the theme
told turning to poem. Will it act
interesting as a page of *National Geographic*

featuring Niger's Wodaabe tribesmen, masters
of the sexy glance, who prize male beauty
in the Sahara super-arid desert?

You were sexy, Ted, big hands, cracked voice,
good heart— a tenor, I assume. With teeth
you could have been anything: baseball

commissioner, short-order cook, male lead
in *Tristan and Isolde.* You used to be you,
a beard in bed, the voice in a bad movie.

Like my father you're remembered, October 8,
1983, and it's annoying as a foot asleep,
pink ocean on a map, or a phone call

on vacation telling me you're dead.

For Daily Use

"A goddess of misfortune,
a myth of perpetual youth.
Stop." is what my telegram read
and why I later said
October was a punitive drink.
Coffee and landscapes,
beards and towers all aching
for the bewilderment of November.
An old woman rested her panic
at a smoky intersection.
I requested the blue highway
on which a march played incessantly
like Disney rehearsing a revolution . . .
It is December. The day travels
with sagging nylons. Unlike the tension
of barking for violence in spring.
Short hours in which to learn
the discreet balance of breath,
what lies beyond it,
and what whispers "hemisphere"
always in autumn.

To the Reader

Let's be lucid as paper on an empty beach.
I'll float to sea in a bottle.
A retired alchemist, you'll lose yourself
to the baser things. I know your foolishness,
your frivolity, investing your grandmother's
fortune in kites. From birth I was serious.
I carried a briefcase to nursery school
and faced the mirror to pray. It led to this
philosophy: erase what you write within two hours.
First wait for the smoke to clear, a cooling off.
And when you're tired of listening to me,
we'll go to the aquarium to hear the soprano
sing to the sharks: it's a lovely song.

from

Japan

Neigh

Smile
  eyelash
oddly toyed
  flourish entered
aimless
     blue
light leaning
  firm to dampen
nascent
  victim
"brings out best"
  birthmarked sofa
garden peeling
  lively draft
or "call it Whistler"
  richness stippled
comet's steel
  palm the grief
for titled
  masses
false trees
  jostling
anxious awful
  half-mad chalk
to backdrop
lazy
  heaven

Strand of
  me
  bright bearded
coast
  a middle distance
close
  a stuttered
semaphore
    conjured grace
in every
never
feather strenuous
  forecast white
  so seer
implacable
  geese and offspring
faithless
  never mind
a wicker
  swimmer
brusque if courtly
  miles to empty
some tempter
  whitened
gauge
last masque
a mote

Paste

Saucy mister
  miserly
    "what you say"
sir
  a decree
close-lipped
  anyhow
willingly cloth
  leopard planet
seething
  drum Satie to go
  artsy saint
age old
    bray
straddle weary
  "Father," he cried
bison eyeballed
  overnight
affaire *de piranha*
  twice drifted
back talk
  throttle
fable
  stuccoed
gauntly
  answering
self-pity

Quick

Sick
   music
shapes wrinkling
    shanty firm
  to altar
    blood
  career
   hysteric
  call if lost
   losing sudden
  Pyrenees
    and doubled
stature
  without knowing
    stairways me
  post breath
amass a Europe
   of old men
     indolent clouding
      trilogy
yourself
  to barter
neurasthenic
   disobeyed
as flapping
  doll-like
thrusts

Shit
  nor merde
secretly
  frightening
harrumph
  on Mars
to ermine
  "the royal couple"
Carlos
  alone in Pennsylvania
wet sailor
  entered
sallow
  clinging
catacomb
  pity music
wooden cages
  Acme, Darling
underneath
  or separately
leaf by leaf
  stiffens
wettest
  icehouse
pigeons toss
    a blithe indifference
upward

Stupidly
   listing
gauzy
    gray
"Today is Friday"
   aquatic Norway
netted
   empires
seclude
    museum's zeroes
"still alive"
   so
frisked and living
   fealty
to cardboard
   shanty
angry
    hell-bent
baroness
   "let's dance"
then
    suicide
       dulcet
    Cadillacs
liquidly
    mental
leanings

Soon a tangle
  a handle
comb
   calmly aluminum
of letter S
  a sign
a shuffle
   sway and swarm
and
   taking shelter
counting backwards
   explosive purple
in remission
   call it
helpless
   lustre
chilly
   first a
tippler
   yelping
yourself
   skyward
waning
   past
succession
   rest it

Since folded
  mirrors
behind its
  mapping
heroes succeed
    so simply
severed
  in heaven
ants
  'will to truth'
metaphoric
    chain saws
surely
  middling
gift-wrapped
  Zeno
apple
  to loathe
nor argued
  imagined
houses
    puzzling
letters trees
and patient
  we go
rootless
  whole

Venus

Sham
　in Occident
orange
　and sunless
fisheye
　anxious
spinal
　laughter
lip service
　usual
to the czar
　"it's camp"
ing
　gallop guzzle
inhale
　boredom
thankless
　sizzling
daylight
　lizard
degree
　drowsy
and if
　stars (backwards)
curtail
　lava
likewise

Waxed

Savannah spendthrift
  fully
me
  wink of
wave
  or larkspur
naked April
  millions
jazzy
  and wingless
nowhere
  mapped a Wednesday
barefoot
  doubt
   a comb
alone
  arrival
roosted
  hopeful
without north
  no bruise
or blindly
  celluloid
waiting
  smoke and
lynx light
  bungling

Swollen
   wrinkle
ridgidly
 joyous
"the whole operation"
  guaranteed
German
   hammer
serious army
  sways
    to growing
    "it's a gusher"
(Texan for Rilke)
   or
breezing
  between
   deadly speeches
fishless
  featureless
purely
  muted
    joy in ending
lest we
  splendor
anxious
  letter
closed

Yeast

Sadness
  anonymous
southern
  air
to run
  a painted
trebled
  feather
rightly
  plenty
cold facts
  serve
up after
  listening oddly
pearled
  nausea
next door
  fella
greenish
  lazy
half-beat
  faster
milky
  maybe silk
old grievance
  ruin the rapids
  will they

Sun
  shut Wednesday
swank of
  missing
ball-point
  dodger
radiant mud
  moving
poor
 a quiet
lapse
  austerely
yours
  endured colossal
sleep
  to reckon
bliss by
  curtained
hearty
  thinness
child's word
  wavers
thinking world
  to open
languor's
  naked
door

New Poems

How Lies Grow

The first time I lied to my baby, I told him that it was his face on the baby food jar. The second time I lied to my baby, I told him that he was the best baby in the world, that I hoped he'd never leave me. Of course I want him to leave me someday. I don't want him to become one of those fat shadows who live in their mother's houses watching game shows all day. The third time I lied to my baby I said, "Isn't she nice?" of the woman who'd caressed him in his carriage. She was old and ugly and had a disease. The fourth time I lied to my baby, I told him the truth, I thought. I told him how he'd have to leave me someday or risk becoming a man in a bow tie who eats macaroni on Fridays. I told him it was for the best, but then I thought, I want him to live with me forever. Someday he'll leave me: then what will I do?

Stories

A few months ago I wrote a story about my sister turning forty though it really wasn't my sister turning forty but a different woman with the vague outlines of my sister. Were the two to meet, I doubt they'd have much to say to each other. They might exchange nervous glances, acknowledging the awkwardness of their age, as old people, I imagine, do on park benches. Yet, when my sister reads the story she might tell me I'm all wrong about what it's like to be forty and that I should hold my peace.

I sent the story to a woman's magazine that had published a previous story of mine about a woman turning thirty-five and finding herself unmarried. The editor, who loved the new story, sent it to her superior, who rejected it on the basis that average readers of the magazine, women between twenty and twenty- five, wouldn't be concerned with the problems of maturity. I perversely wondered whether I might change the ages of the couple involved but stopped short of revision, realizing that the characters were definitely "mature." I even thought of retitling the story "Maturity" for spite but remembered Conrad's lyrical tribute called "Youth" and left my story alone.

Meanwhile, painters were busy in our flat, turning everything "document," a color between blue and gray. One day when it was very hot and they were sweating over the fireplace, a young man from Gary, Indiana, dropped over unexpectedly, manuscript in hand. He had heard my husband give a poetry reading and wanted Paul to hear some of his poems. Paul suggested that the young poet simply leave the manuscript, but the man insisted on reading the poems out loud, dramatically, in the presence of he painters, who couldn't help but listen. The painters agreed with Paul that the one about the Indian on the postage stamp was his best.

It was Don who ventured the opinion about the poems. He was the more helpful of the two painters. One day he carried my groceries up forty-seven stairs to the third floor and insisted on leaving them in the kitchen at the far end of the flat. His partner John was silent, smaller and less obtrusive. In fact, he'd wear shirts to match the color of the room he was painting. On the day that he was doing "document," he wore a lovely blue surgeon's smock. I asked him what he'd wear when he did our wallpaper, since our kitchen was to be done in a graph paper design of blue, cinnamon, and brown on a beige background. On the sweltering wallpapering day, he wore no shirt at all. He laughed at my serious desire to know how people make these small decisions.

Throughout the week my husband and I acknowledged the painters' presence by speaking more politely to each other than we usually do. Finally, I imagined that the painters might move in with us. We could host daily salons where they could review young poets' work. Of course, it would also be fair for the poets to criticize the work of the painters. Since Don and John have gone, I've noticed lapses of their attention, particularly in their rendition of a beige kitchen door.

The story about my sister takes place in California, where she lives, and features versions of her friends, though if they read it, they'd be wise enough not to recognize themselves. The husband in the story is also not my sister's husband but a flatter substitute. Round and flat characters, so loved by high school English teachers, no longer appeal to us as a critical notion. Many characters seem trapezoidal. All I mean by the use of flat is that he, like most people on paper, underwent a cooling process, what a printer achieves in reproducing Van Gogh in black and white.

My sister herself is a technically good painter but has never known what to paint. Often she chooses slides of vacation landscapes to reproduce, as if art can only occur two thousand miles from home. The boats have proper reflections and one can discern a storm brewing in the lackluster sky. Still, I wonder why she never chooses to paint what's around her. In her garden are a variety of slugs and snails that leave silvery trails on her redwood deck. Their shine on wood might make a good painting, but I imagine it never occurs to her.

Our front room looks better in document than it did in off-white. The walls have been forced to cohere and provide a conscious setting for the art we hang there. One of our etchings is of a man's face emerging from shadow. My mother once mistook it for a black and gray sunset, which is what she conceives art to be. My cousin, who makes huge photographs of mountains and seaside, warped in Mylar reflections, especially likes that etching, so unlike her own work, and a woman with a very fine art collection mistook it for a Rouault. Of course, I was mildly worried, hoping that the artist hadn't intended his etching to be mistaken for a Rouault, as an artificial flower excellently rendered might be sniffed again and again. Paul's father once thought the etching to be an outline of West Virginia, the state where he first practiced the ministry. We assured him that it wasn't. He looked discouraged and insisted anyway on telling us his West Virginia stories, of rhubarb pies served cut in halves, of locust honey representing the state at the 1939 World's Fair, and of women fainting in dark revival tents.

If my sister reads the story, she may find that she likes the flat and predictable husband better than her own. I'll remind her it is not her husband but a slide of him with the light slightly wrong and dust streaming through the blinds.

Wall Decorations

1

My daughter draws a self-portrait, brown squiggles for hair, obscure mouse body, feet the shape of Arizona. "That's nice," I tell her and ask for some more pictures I can use to decorate the fluorescent walls of my green institutional office. Within the next hour, she's created twenty such drawings, all of herself. Each time her hair is awkwardly tangled, feet enlarged, body almost absent.

2

On his thirty-fourth birthday, my friend goes to a specialty store to purchase his first sports coat in thirty-four years. He chooses herringbone because he's never seen second hand herringbone at the Salvation Army. Buying the coat, he jokes about how it makes him respectable for funerals. Now that he's nearly thirty-five, he imagines the imminent death of friends. The salesman shows him a melon-pink jacket that's going to Florida that very weekend. "My own," the salesman says, pointing to the wide lapels, "will never again be in style." My friend nods politely. He doesn't know how he's lived through so many awkward situations without a sports coat.

3

I'm sitting in my office before class, noticing how my plants have been drowned over Christmas vacation by an overzealous janitor. My office decorations amount to four identical self- portraits of my daughter and photos of several friends. One of my typically polite Vietnamese students sidles in, rigidly smiling. "What is it, Tran?" I ask. He needs a missed assignment. "Are those your children?" he asks, pointing to the identical scrawls on my wall. "No," I answer, addressing his use of the plural. "Is that your husband?" he asks me of the serious man in the herringbone sports coat. "No, Tran," I say. "Thank you, Teacher," he answers, bowing as he leaves.

My God, Louis
Zukofsky, how awful
you look on the back
of the turquoise book
the color of booths
in diners. Though
reading your poems
consoles me. I'd
like to write without
punctuation but I need
a sign that I'm still
breathing, dashes
leading to more— it
isn't easy to ignore
the need for signs.
Once on a road in
the dark I was afraid.
I couldn't read
the signs: Of course
I was drunk and twenty
and driving with some
friends. We stopped
and I had pancakes.
I'd ruined Holly's
party by taking a walk
with her boyfriend,
who liked my breasts
so much it made me
sick. So it was motor-
cycle rides all night
and breakfast dates.
I got Mono not from
kissing but from lack
of sleep. Which is

why I like your poems:
Nothing is needed like
stained glass light. If
breasts are in them,
fine. If not, goodnight.

Nausea

I felt it first in a gallery
where the paintings were large
and foolish. Something about
Noah's Ark encased in blood
and the lives of lizards
in a triptych of feathery
gray snakes. I thought I'd
go cross-eyed or even faint,
shocking Koren, who was doing
cartwheels, and Kenward, who
was not. Imagine your mother/
friend prone at an exhibit,
having to stand over her
stupid presumed anguish.
I'd read at the airport that
59% of all Americans have
phobias, more women included
than men. I've observed my
fear of whispering, which has
nothing to do with people
telling secrets but with feeling
that I'm just waking up into something
I don't fully understand.
In "Vertigo," of course, he stands
on stepladders to cure his
tragic flaw that even killed
when the hand slipped out of
reach. Will they say
of me, "You can't trust her
in galleries. Don't show
her art"? I'm not afraid
of swimming or the cab ride
back from Brooklyn with
the Godfather's godchildren,

speedometer up to eighty
in the otherwise boring tunnel.
We laughed so hard I thought
we'd gone Chinese. Now there's
a topic for fear. Red hordes
in the cities, parachuted in,
like the dream I had in 1968,
when I was in love with Eugene McCarthy.
He saved me in the end though
the world got destroyed.
I'm afraid of large extinct birds
in the cases of the Natural
History Museum. I don't mind
the hooded mummies at the place,
but I can feel the talons and hear
wings. I'm not afraid of flying
but of imagining other lives
I might lead, like postcards
of a gallery I'd like to visit
where the paintings are beautiful and
small and analogous to singing.

Monday

Insolvent and green, tending to
swarm, the waves' gray flags have
inchworm insignias: convertibles,
ether, shiny gloves and whole notes.

Like a photograph of the circus,
the reds and moon blues are convincing.
The yellow cul-de-sac is too familiar.
How terrible that it repeats itself.

Dreadlocks on the president. Him
no good at mathematics. A blur
of possibility arranges itself like
a season in the chauffeur's mirror.

Fabulous clouds are not trivial.
On the rose-covered parade float,
starlets arrange themselves like
anchors in a kicking sea. *Ouch!*

"Beware how she scratches," meaning
the baby. Pink fuzz soldiers stand
guard. Father phones in his deciding
vote. Serious and shrill, baby nods.

The blue pillbox said Monday. Ianthe
shrugged and stirred her Ceylonese
tea. White smiles glinted like seagulls.
She pressed a carnation and mailed her purse.

The plot thickened. Involving an Egyptian
chanteuse, Marx and Engels, George and Gracie,
purple stationery and a Swiss bank account.
History was reshaped precisely at noon.

You are the first passenger to have
survived Italy. A bronze plaque will be
purchased in you honor, saluting your
eyelids, ardor, sins and wry humor.

Leap Year Day

The paleolithic heart might burst
with news of slowness, news of feathers.
All the softness listed in the register
you keep: day of finite crashing.
Who's to say the deafness that you wore
was needed by the Greeks? Depression
sounded like a whole note sewn with
lilac thread. I wanted to assure you
that the small biology of kissing
would not last until the last pebble dried
and a flag wobbled and a list faded and a map
was drawn and a green planet drifted
under your lens. The elbowed dawn lifted,
and you said nothing of the storm that flashed
off-shore, as if to mean, forgotten winter
without signs. You will not fade.
I believe your wholeness as it rests its future
on our lengthening half-lit letters.

He Said Goodbye

Don Quixote was his favorite disease.
He was only ten, when, in Florence,
the Blue Sweaters took away his mother.
He'd never been taught to cough so.
1949: "My hands have grown so large!
La Rue de la False View!" He blue-
pencilled the inconsistencies: That
it wasn't 1949, that he couldn't pass
water, that the snow was anachronistic,
falling like giant lotto balls. "LK," he said,
"meet KL," but unconvincingly. He read,
"Key Largo Left Lawless by Loan Sharks,"
and made a strong tea. He felt
a chronic sense of having won.
A manifesto came to him, a flawless middle
age, much rustling in the field
of red scarves. He was bilingual.
He sang in Portuguese, "A Yoyoist
from Yonkers." He had no boyhood
favorites. When the weinstube closed,
a dinghy passed, the color of his hair.
The afternoon was yellow like morphine.

Hangar: Harangue

She was dressed for heaven
when she entered the room,
her harelip harem escape
a legend in her culture.
She was hard-headed.
She was hardy. Her name
was not and had never been
Harold. "Have some hashish?"
she asked in general.
The general had been wounded.
His arm hung disarmingly from
his sleeve. No one would have
guessed that his hatband
was holy, that his haunch
was itchy, that his hawk's
beard had died of overwatering.
She was abundantly nourished
by his Hebrew side. A highball
or two touched haggard lips.
"Why, this is hilarious," she
said of his hospice where he'd
taken himself to have a hot
toddy or two before the war
started up again like an old
movie they'd both seen before.
"I think we have the same hosier,"
he said when he kissed her.
Then Hypnos descended like
hyphens and ended their history.

Found on a Bedside Table

"Vague as twilight rowing.
Built to satisfy the czar
before the serious army
debarked from their shadow-
tank. Their mission:
to change the wallpaper
to discreet begonias
without the help of
professionals. Not that
leather can give: pink
cows vanish in a field
of magnetic force. Which
may explain what happened
when monuments were placed
in a diagram denoting taxes.
Now I drizzle, seeing my
last lament waiting like
a moist traveler. *But*
is not useful when a measured
language is desired like a
birdwatcher's migration manual.
I have forced the focus back
to you. Having previously
exhausted your exploits with
G. (though admittedly austere
and lacking the fullness of
oceans), I will be brief.
Our summer on the traffic
island will not be scrutinized.
I can no longer make out
the color of your hair or the
song we sang like a rough
calypso. Tell me the myth
of swimming applies to the

smallest understanding of
our fits. We were lopsided.
Like a humorous gesture on
an airplane to Mecca. Now I
count the notes between ice
cream trucks and remember
the smell of stoplights,
the underside of your chin,
needlemarks on the oranges
we bought from the bearded
Serbian terrorist who told us
once, 'You belong in neon.'"

Isms

1

Myself
 though armor
itself
 like maps
of pigeons
 overhand
ledger's
 sleeping
 she
not Milton
 moonlit feather
bellows stellar
 smaller i
patient
 royal
limitless
 dejeuner
learned
 to purring
kabuki
 workhouse
love to silk
 a sorry England
together weathered
 droll
not wings
 of rural afterwards
letters rumored

                singing eyeballed
        her

                    2
        Spring
        up
                near a concave
        undershirt
                it is not

        antidote
                for living
        until a given time
                when
        chanteuse in French
                    is recent
        reaching
                a point preordained
        a mission
                    engulfed
        nor
            express permit to enter-
        tain a possible
                futurity
        vulcanized tulips
                whips curl
        an ad for beauty
                a salt
        Hart Crane's
                galoshes
        sink of swim
            mechanical hearts

3

Bless Celeste
　　whose asking
waned riper
　　not victory
　　no
plain leopard
　　whose Nebraska
is recent
　　& whole (no superlative)
silky separatist
　　under glass
a task
　　of the air
for measure
　　reveals a coast
not hers
nor radial prime mover

　　ancient narcissus
asks only
　　　of guess
to own
　　or levy
itchy memorial
　　to between the hop
the Ganges grill
　　feathered
　　　hopeless
(Diesel
　　the man
whose confab
　　called a "maiden over"
mainly if
　　a minced inch measured)

4

Spleen
　　　and patience
patent wink
　　latent angel
burst a likely
　　trance
coupling
　　rooted
burning
　　no
drowsy ears
　　enter
languid season
　　listless workings
　　　　ionized
air
　　framed in
rumor
　　frivolous mother
　　　　lasting
　　frenzy
"A" train panic
　　last to leave
ballast
　　deadweight league
Ripper challenged
　　hourly

Token

1

Collaborative fire
in arboreal sky.
A black Eden
in a golden age,
a recklessness
we forsake
when breathing takes
its web inside.
We couldn't see
the flowers,
the dependent scenery.
You wanted more lines
in the play you directed
when a brisk immobility
grasped your skull
in public. Lidded
grief was close
to such a noise
but no eclipse
could fix its mirror
on the stem of heart
you called a scanning.
Yellow was left out,
and you were drawn
through bliss to
this alive cold reckoning.

2

Haloed by December,
suddenly it's May.
A sealed-off vacation,
a mind sweep. Never saw
the new money depicting
health spas for swans.
The turnstile is stuck
and deco-addicts leave
their terra-cotta sky
motifs on my dusty pillared past.
Pardon my getting lost
in the simplest sentence,
a stumbling magnet
out for a bronze promenade.
Shun the crowd that forms
to see the Duke escape
each night at eight o'clock.
What's inside the gunny sack
he carries? A taboo added
to passion, the ill-gotten
season on the dew-line.

3

You call it a restive satisfaction
for those who want miracles
in small-case letters.
Why not dignify our pallor?
You want a bowl of pears
whose contours never ripen,
some somber cannon smoke
reminding
us of loss. Cultivated grief,
to know our fingers touch
what we own separately

as if to say I crown you each
with logic, lengthening your shapes
to serve what I imagine.

For My Father

(1915-1974)

He was my face on a necessary white
Summers surfacing to clean his eyes
A word printed blue
under and above breath
Hands frozen through the radio
Names were burst adrift
Enlarge my hands repeating "dizziness"
Stairs shine yellow and talkative
Black planets are replacing desire
Two monks humming "I" dark like medicine

Always twelve ticks saying good-bye
Wings opening, talking back
My own body closing its cells
Occan posed in a downpour
for a world of colorful funerals

One poetry, false subjects
The third floor drawls "house"
A woman points to an angel's past tense
Summer ties a skull to its absence
The zero of rowboats' unseen circles

Should I?

Blue blurred continent,
green kicking curves,
altitude where no one
wears hats or measures
rain. Shall I grow
pathetic with mouths,
graze the leafy fields
of Africa, carry water
from a steaming well?
Shall I be a building
with portico? I'll
compose my list of
heroes: girth of the
entire circus, leaden
thickness of statues,
zoo walrus filled with
herring swallowed whole,
topiary shrubs resembling
planets. I am miles from
their aesthetic, the proper
middle distance where it's
cool as November. In
my bloated gown I'll smile,
prom queen posed with peonies
dripping ants. What do
I want anyway? To be the
eighth day of creation, Ann
Boleyn's Sunday underwear,
a teenage mummy in a base-
ment crypt? Thin is a word
and anonymous as circumference
minus my painterly flesh and
hopeful wedge of cheekbones
shadowing my new reticence.

Round for Four Voices

for K.E.

Lugubrious lunchpails!
What is good is also
murderous. Thin-lipped
to nothingness, he dotes.
Drafty luminous deserts.
Not like your comic
cataracts of sensibility.

Boffo, the secretive one.
Spells his name in eels.
Plays sound-effects at
funerals. Ordered a black
grape arbor. Shirl says
he's a genius. Caligula's
cousin's aunt's step-uncle.

Worser than Wichita.
Man-boot-cigar feverish.
X-ray cocktail lounge.
Ahoy, pianists sink ships.
Terrible glaciers' utterly
icy hauteur. Baby weights
and lipsticked lion breath.

Diet of planets and rooms.
Unlit spaces poppied with
scarves. Skinny untouch-
able stockings hung out.
Alps from airplane wing.
Swallow the christening
water. Fat red theater.

Poised

A stick of dogwood from a
Georgia swamp is wrapped
in yesterday's *Korean Times*,
$1.99, while the florist
rings up my sale, chanting
"Easter coming, Easter
coming." Koren asks,
"Why Easter?" She doesn't
believe in it: "Oh, sure!"
to the Resurrection. Real
miracles are ungainly as
Raymond Burr in *Ironsides*
overflowing his wheelchair
or rivers bulging in spring
with dogs on top of garages
and frantic music from
the Orpheum Movie Theater.
I reread Hemingway. He's
crazier than I'd remembered,
but his simple declarations
are slow and reassuring:
"The town was very nice
and our house was very fine."
A word for everything leaves
the door ajar in the fact
of being me like cold red
spring on Mars or walking
on an ice-locked lake, slipping
along like art: hesitation
meant to hold a calm.

Chicago Symphony

We sleep to Sibelius
and the tousled
pianist's careful—
is it Mozart? Crunch
some Pastillines, mouth
music keeping us alive.
Now the guest conductor's
off and better for it.
He's won the honor
at an auction, works at
Gucci and is scared,
conducting stiffly as
cartoon clockhands.
Down the aisle French
is spoken. Should we
vacation there or howl
at the moonless rotund
ceiling? I remember
Frank Kovacic's air-
filled satin sleeves
when he'd go off on Sat-
urday's to play polkas
for South Side Croatian
weddings, birthdays,
wakes. And Agnes Lustig,
who played the harp
and worked at A & P.
I'll touch your knee
to rouse my sense of
sense. Or cough to make
a joke. The pounding
elsewhere pressure does
go on: slow and slow
as the onstage kettle drum.

Trees in pairs can't
lead a life like ours.

Measuring

We're watching the sad movie
for the seventh time today.
Let's take off our tear-vial
glasses and observe: Like
yawns, tears travel the
audience, dumb tears,
Cockney tears, red, white
and blue tears, touching-
only-to-his-mother tears.
Leaky tear valves fill
the Potomac. Frenchmen
cry into their berets.
Children cry on metal decks
of ocean liners. I'd like
to cry with you for just
one minute, five short of
the national average for
women, but then again I'm no
average woman. We could
conquer television with our
true emotions, make announcers
weep and ad executives foam
like geysers. I'll cry over
the burned English muffin
on my plate. You'll cry
into the sink. What are
tears like? Variety shows,
doorkeepers who've lost
their keys, mother-in-laws
naked, a shabby church
where a madonna is said
to have wept last Tuesday.
We lose patience with our
own grand gestures. We are

left with one memento,
the saddest of them all,
our desire to emote like
factory chimneys in December.

The Apology Store

I needed an all-purpose apology for the many occasions
I had surely forgotten and was to forget. It could be
vague and unshaped as the future or distinct as a map of
the ancestral country printed in Braille. My funds were
unlimited, my purpose a banner of good intentions.

"We're sorry," they said, "but currency won't do."

"I have small bills and large," I chirped.

"American or foreign currencies aren't accepted. We're
sorry."

"Then charge one of each and gift-wrap them, please."
Even if I staggered under a pile tall as Jacob's ladder, I'd
get them to the car.

"Our spring line is sold out and our summer line is
threatened by numerous strikes. It's touch and go.
We're..."

"Sorry," I finished, a little short of my usual good cheer.
Perhaps I could leave my name. You could call when a
few arrive. What with strikes by anchor-forgers, spinach-
choppers and midwives, I can understand your troubles
and I'm . . ."

"Sorry you're having them," the clerk chimed. He bore
an uncanny resemblance to my grandfather, so I
decided to appeal on familial lines. I shed a single
theatrical tear. I waved my arms like a *Perpetuum
Mobile* at a departure gate. The clerk remained station-
ary.

Down on my knees, I asked for a promise: "Will you call me when your supply is shipped?" Now he looked like the yellow cocker spaniel I lost at a Sunday school picnic forty years ago.

"I'm sorry," he said. "We don't have a phone.

Ones: white for purity. A white man says his prayers in a white room. White nightshirt. White hair. In the background (raised velveteen relief) is an altar. Impaled on a stalagmite: the old money. "Self-reference is our motto" is reflected in a real mirror shaped like the continental forty-eight. Squint and you can see the Rockies. Cost: $49.98, discounted for summer white sale.

Fives: Colossal black olives rest in a bed of generals and wanted men who appear agitated, anonymous as canned goods. They are the first designer bills with Salvador Dali's signature in gold leaf. There's a run on the Chase Manhattan as they are bought up by counter-agents trying to strengthen the zloty. They are duplicated by forgers in developing nations where unemployed Ph.D.'s are used as cheap labor. Finally replaced by Norman Rockwell money, familiar and comfortable. Nobody wants to steal it.

Tens: out of circulation. Fear of decimals in high places. The president sleeps with mittens and wingtips. What more can be said of the intimate nature of currency?

Thirteens: largest of bills. Featuring football fields, battleships named after women in the thirties, hair fetishes, arenas where flamenco dancers practice voluntary metabolism. Reverse side: an appeal to sentiment. Paw raised in a friendly salute, everyone's favorite pet is quoted (in Latin) as saying, "I am snowing on your capital, a lost Caravaggio, a taxidermist's dream of islands in relief."

The Moe, Larry and Curly Conspiracy

Can a woman, despite her chromosomal destiny,
like the Three Stooges? Will Nancy Drew
decipher the message the widow left
in the steam writing on her teacup?
Should the Bobbsey twins give their aunt
the needle? "Where were you when Kennedy
was shot?" the toupeed newsman asks.
I was in Miss Gallagher's French class
looking up her skirt. (She sat that way.)
And Bonny, the bedwetter who smelled
of Mary Janes, said it was a flesh wound.
My sister came home from college, and we went
to the empty Avalon Theater and saw the *VIP's*,
in which Elizabeth Taylor shared an airport
penthouse with Richard Burton. We rode home
in my sister's Studebaker, the color of toast
with jelly, and my sister cried. I thought
shit fuck piss on JFK for making her so sad.

Maybe a Comedian?

Can a woman be sexy in earmuffs?
The man on Johnny Carson told
Aristotelian jokes. They deconstructed
until the commercial re/frozen pancakes.
I know one about an ape who goes to a
bar. I won't tell it for fear my cigar
will go out. Napoleon jokes are a hit
in solitary confinement. Samuel Johnson
is never funny. Can Henry Cabot Lodge
be a punchline? Can square-jawed?
Even in India there is a class clown.
We like our comedians sad, our heroes
inwardly dull as burning logs.
Here's a stamp of the man who coined
the phrase, "Hold the mustard!"
a saying cherished by the gods who are
never funny but awe us with their
Spiro Agnew impressions on Presidents'
Day and their cheap lightning in the middle
of the Right-to-Life parade and picnic.

The Sentimental

for Max Ernst

Eros, the power neither
gods nor man resists,
smiles on the ermine,
a weasel so sublime
it wears a white hair shirt.
The Coup de Grâce Award
is offered by the Sacred Order
of the Sentimental Spleen
to the artist who's designed
a bridge of wet begonias.
Gallantly he twice refuses.
("Ambition should be made
of sterner stuff.") Today
the Eiffel Tower bends
arthritic girders,
an old man picking leeks.
The Arc de Triomphe stops
its entrance with a cork.
Plaster cabs must idle
while their drivers
show their sequined edicts:
"In mourning for his death,
all bridges must wear lace."

The Twittering Machine

We were not in possession of ourselves
when we went to the carnival.
Round colors imploded until a clock
unwinding in a drawer became the most
real instrument of pleasure. Madness
drove away most customers, and the lines
were ludicrously short. Yes, it was empty
at the attic, at the window ledge,
at the doors of our token security.
"Knowledge," we heard someone on
the bumper cars say, "is a shiny raincoat."
On the ferris wheel we often saw
the needles of history pierce one or more
gray balloons. It was sad, it was indirect,
it was sheer autocracy when a pocket of sympathy
opened for us that night and something stepped
inside quietly. Now and then we flog
the air, hoping to repossess it.

April Fools'

What I liked best
wasn't that Yo-Yo Ma played
his cello at Carnegie Hall,
or that I jumped back
from the World's Largest
Television as though I'd burned
my hand. The bow-legged man
in the park made me think
of punctuation,
slow and lyrical as spring.
The Early Warning System buzzed
the TV screen while I made
coffee: Oh good, the end of
the world. Then told my mother
we'd have lunch at two.
Happy April Fools',
Professor Wayne C. Booth,
who claims our use of irony
shows our fear of God
the Father not liking
his smirking children.
As the robot-washer sprayed
my car, I thought
the word "adhesive" deserves
more credit, like Dean Martin
for making Jerry Lewis funny.
Our serious selves should
try at times to please:
"That spider in your hair,
Madame?" It's really there
and open to analysis,
the pretense of surprise
that lights the day with color.